Favorite Fairy Tales
TOLD IN JAPAN

Favorite Fairy Tales

TOLD IN JAPAN

Retold by Virginia Haviland

Illustrated by Carol Inouye

A Beech Tree Paperback Book 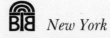 *New York*

First Beech Tree Edition, 1996, published by arrangement with Little, Brown and Co.
Printed in the United States of America

10 9 8 7 6 5 4 3 2

Library of Congress Cataloging-in-Publication Data

Haviland, Virginia, 1911–1988
      Favorite fairy tales told in Japan / retold by Virginia Haviland ; illus-
trated by Carol Inouye.
            p.   cm.
      Originally published: Boston : Little, Brown & Co., 1967.
      Summary: Five traditional Japanese tales: "One-inch Fellow," "The Good
Fortune Kettle," "The Tongue-Cut Sparrow," "Momotaro," and "The White Hare
and the Crocodiles."
      ISBN 0-688-12601-4 (pbk.)
      1. Fairy tales — Japan.   [1. Fairy tales.   2. Folklore — Japan.]
    I. Title.
    PZ8.H295Favl 1996
    398.21'0952—dc20   94–3079
                                                              CIP
                                                              AC

Minor editorial and style changes have been made in the stories for these new
editions.

These Stories Have Been Retold
From the Following Sources:

"One-Inch Fellow" is retold from *Picture Tales From the Japanese* by Chiyuno Sugimoto. Copyright 1928, 1956 by Chiyuno Sugimoto. (J.B. Lippincott Company).

"The Good Fortune Kettle" is retold from a translation by Matsuyo Yamamoto of the version found in Toshio Iwasaki's *Iwaki Mukashibanashishu* in the series of volumes *Zenkoku Mukashi-banashikiroku*, edited by Kunio Yanagida (Tokyo, Sanseido, 1942, 1942). Kunio Yanagida is the founder of the scientific study of folklore in Japan.

"The Tongue-Cut Sparrow," "Momotaro or The Story of the Son of a Peach," and "The White Hare and the Crocodiles" are retold from *Japanese Fairy Tales*, compiled by Yei Theodora Ozaki (Tokyo, 1904; New York, A. L. Burt, 1905). The preface to this volume states that "this collection of Japanese folk tales is the outcome of a suggestion made to me indirectly through a friend by Mr. Andrew Lang. They have been translated from the modern version written by Sadanami Sanjin. These stories are not literal translations, and though the Japanese story and all the quaint Japanese expressions have been faithfully preserved, they have been told more with the view to interest young readers of the West than the technical student of folklore....In one or two instances I have gathered an incident from another version."

The reteller of these five *Favorite* stories is deeply grateful to Miss Momoko Ishii and Miss Matsuyo Yamamoto of Tokyo for helpful notes regarding versions of stories used, especially concerning details in the Ozaki versions. In retelling "Momotaro" I have followed the more traditional characterizing of the animals as friendly and helpful rather than military, and I have omitted the extraneous introduction of the maidens, not usually found in authoritative versions.

Contents

One-Inch Fellow

One-Inch Fellow

ONCE UPON A TIME there lived an old man and an old woman in the village of Naniwa, which is the present city of Osaka. They were a happy couple, except for one thing. They had no child to cheer their lonely old age.

One afternoon they went to the temple and prayed, "Please, god of mercy, give us a child—any child, even if it be as small as a thumb."

On a summer evening after this, as the old couple were looking up at a beautiful moon, they saw something strange, like a spot of darkness coming at them from the moon. It came nearer and nearer, and soon seemed to them like a dark cloud.

The cloud floated into the room where the old man and old woman were sitting. It twirled and untwirled itself, and quickly wafted away again. The old couple watched in silent wonder and then with great joy, for the cloud had left behind it a tiny boy as small as a thumb.

This gift was received as a miracle by the grateful couple. They soon discovered that the little fellow did not grow bigger as babies do, but they continued to be grateful and to care lovingly for the tiny boy. He remained as small as a thumb, so the old couple named him "One-Inch Fellow."

Whenever One-Inch Fellow ventured out on

the street alone, the good old woman worried. "Old man, old man, what if the children on the street should fight with One-Inch Fellow? He would be crushed!"

But she need not have worried. Whenever the teasing children came toward One-Inch Fellow, he would dart away quick as a flash between their wooden clogs, so that they could not find him.

Fourteen summers went by and One-Inch Fellow was now a young man.

"Honorable Father, honorable Mother," he said one day, bowing low before his parents. They were seated at their low table, which to One-Inch Fellow seemed like a high roof above him.

The old man looked down upon his son. "What is it, my son?"

"I should like your permission to go to the capital of Kyoto to make a name for myself."

"And why is that?" asked the parents in surprise.

"Because I am a grown son now," he answered, lifting his tiny head high. "My gratitude to you is higher than the highest mountains and deeper than the deepest seas. I want to make a name for myself so that you will be proud of me."

The old man looked down. "I give you permission. Go, my son!"

During the next days, the old parents were very busy. The old woman made a new kimono for One-Inch Fellow. "In Kyoto young men dress with style. I shall have my son look his best."

The old man also planned for his son. "He is too small for a real boat. And he must have a sword. No son of mine can step out into the world without a sword."

Early on the day of departure, the old woman was up, cooking over her charcoal fire, while the old man prepared a farewell speech. In silence the three ate their breakfast, and One-Inch

Fellow neatly tied in his little square cloth some newly cooked rice balls and salted plums.

"Honorable parents, I take my leave now," he said, bowing low before them.

"This is your sword," said his father, handing to One-Inch Fellow a shiny, sharp needle in a scabbard of straw. "Keep it always stainless like your soul.

"And this is your boat," added his father, placing a black lacquered soup bowl with one chopstick before him. "Steer it well to Kyoto with this oar. And now go, my son."

Carrying the boat, the parents walked with One-Inch Fellow to the water's edge. The old man put the bowl on the water and helped his son climb into it. With his oar, One-Inch Fellow steered his boat out to the deeper part of the river.

The voices of the old people called after him as he paddled away. *"Banzai! Banzai!"*

The old man continued to wave, but the old woman hid her face in her sleeve.

One-Inch Fellow started thus on his way to a famous career. With his chopstick paddle he pushed on and on. Angry waves sometimes threw him clear off his course. One stormy day he hid behind a support of a bridge and rested until the wind died and there was only a gentle breeze.

Finally one morning early he saw the city of Kyoto rising above the mist. Happily he steered toward shore. He stepped out of his boat, and he pushed it away. "When I return to Naniwa," he said, "I shall have an attendant and shall not need this little boat."

Compared to his quiet home of Naniwa, One-Inch Fellow found the capital big and noisy. He walked briskly down the middle of a wide street where crowds of people passed back and forth. No one noticed so tiny a fellow. After passing several wooden gates, One-Inch

Fellow stopped before the highest and longest walls. "This must be a rich household. I shall offer my services here."

Through the largest gateway he made his way and, walking over a long road, came finally to the entrance of an immense mansion. It belonged to a famous lord of Kyoto. On the great stone step at the door, he saw a pair of shiny painted black shoes. The lord of the mansion was about to go out.

"Hear me!" One-Inch Fellow shouted as loud as he could.

"Who is that?" It was the dignified lord himself who answered.

"It is I, a youth from Naniwa," answered One-Inch Fellow.

The lord came out and looked around, but he could not see anyone.

Again One-Inch Fellow shouted, "Here I am!"

The startled lord looked down at the ground.

"*Yo!* What a tiny fellow; but you have a mighty voice! Who are you?"

"I am called One-Inch Fellow. I have come all the way from Naniwa to serve a great lord."

"*Yo!* I do not know what a little fellow like you could do."

"But," cried One-Inch Fellow, "you will find no other fellow like me on all this earth!"

"That is so! All right, you may serve me," said the lord.

From that day, One-Inch Fellow became a faithful servant to this lord of Kyoto. He was given the duty of cleaning all the shiny lacquered shoes. In his spare moments he never failed to clear away a fallen leaf or a stray pine needle from the mossy ground. Always he was courteous and bright and did willingly any errands asked of him. The whole household liked to call out, "One-Inch Fellow! One-Inch Fellow!" In the servants' hall he became a much sought-after little man.

At length One-Inch Fellow won the attention of the beautiful Princess, who was the only daughter of the lord. He became such a favorite with her, in fact, that the lord permitted him to be her bodyguard. Every winter he went out with her to celebrate the New Year. In the spring he accompanied her to the cherry-blossom festivals; and in summer he shared in the viewing of the full moon. When fall came, One-Inch Fellow escorted the Princess, with other attendants, to the shrine of Ise where every maiden makes a holy pilgrimage at least once before her marriage.

This pilgrimage was such a long journey that One-Inch Fellow sometimes rode in the pocket of another attendant.

After the visit to the shrine, the Princess—with One-Inch Fellow and her other attendants behind her—came down a long, shadowy avenue of cedar trees. Suddenly a huge monster, an *Oni,* leaped out of the darkness, yelling, *"Wa—! Wa—!"*

At the sight of this ugly Oni, the beautiful Princess screamed and fainted away, while the terrified attendants ran off in different directions to hide. Only tiny One-Inch Fellow stood his ground.

"What are you?" he shouted, standing before the Princess. "Do you know who I am!" he cried, looking up to the fierce Oni. "I am the famous One-Inch Fellow who serves the great lord of Kyoto. This is his only daughter. If you even so much as come near her, beware!"

"Ha! Ha! Ha! I like to hear you talk!" laughed the huge Oni, looking down at the tiny man. "But that is enough. Do not bother me, or I shall eat you up!"

"Yoshi! Go ahead," cried One-Inch Fellow, angrily.

As One-Inch Fellow expected, the huge monster caught hold of him, and started to put him into his huge mouth. Quickly One-Inch Fellow darted onto his cheek. He climbed up to the monster's eye, whipped out his needle sword, and thrust it at the eye.

"*Itai!* Ouch!" cried the monster, trying to catch him. But One-Inch Fellow slipped from the monster's fingers and went on thrusting his needle sword all over the Oni's face.

"No more! No more!" roared the monster. "I make my humble bow to you!"

One-Inch Fellow quickly ran down to the ground and the Oni disappeared into the shadows. By this time the Princess had opened her eyes. "What happened to the Oni?" she asked.

"I have chased him away with my sword. Do not worry, Princess. One-Inch Fellow, your bodyguard, is at your service."

Then the Princess exclaimed, "What is that?"

A few feet away lay a large wooden hammer.

"That must be something the monster left behind," said One-Inch Fellow. "If you are rested, let us hasten homeward."

"Wait!" cried the Princess, lifting up the hammer. "Stand there, One-Inch Fellow. This looks like a magic hammer that can answer wishes. That monster must have been a god in disguise who came to test you. Otherwise he would not have left behind this precious hammer."

"May I ask, Princess, how you know that is such a wonderful gift?"

"We shall see," said the Princess solemnly. One-Inch Fellow had never seen the Princess so solemn.

"If this be the magic hammer my honored father has spoken of, then when you strike it, anything you wish will come true. What do you wish, One-Inch Fellow? Speak!"

"I have nothing to wish for since my wish has been granted. I am serving your honored father. Still—perhaps I might like to be a little taller."

"Please, merciful god, make One-Inch Fellow tall as a man." The Princess said this very quietly, and struck the hammer on the ground.

Strange! Strange! One-Inch Fellow seemed to see the earth sinking lower and lower. But it was not the earth that was changing; it was he who was growing taller.

"Please, merciful god, make him tall as a man," the Princess said, as she struck the hammer a second time.

As she repeated this for the third time, the Princess smiled at One-Inch Fellow. She lifted the hammer into the air and let it fall to the ground again with a heavy thud.

The beautiful Princess now went over to her little traveling box which an attendant had thrown down before he ran away. From it she

took a round mirror, which she held toward One-Inch Fellow. Looking into the mirror, he saw that he was tall! The Princess lifted the mirror higher and higher so that he could see himself all the way from the tips of his feet to his manly face. He was not merely tall, he was magnificent, a full six feet!

With joy in their hearts, the Princess and the tall youth returned to her father's mansion. For saving the life of his precious daughter, the lord promoted the lad to a high rank, while the cowardly attendants who had fled at the sight of the monster resigned from their positions in great shame. News of the brave youth who had saved the life of the Princess became gossip in every corner of the court. Finally the heroic story even reached the gracious ears of the Emperor, and the youth was immediately summoned before him. The Emperor bestowed a high title on One-Inch

Fellow, and not long after gave him an honorable position.

Before three full moons had passed, the youth dressed in his full court regalia and went to see his honored parents. Behind him on the journey followed his attendants and two palanquins which were to carry his parents back to the beautiful home which the youth had built for himself in Kyoto. The old couple were made very happy, sharing the honors of their son. But they were happy, above all, because the youth was no longer as tiny as a thumb. Their old feet were never too weary to take them to the temple to offer their prayers of gratitude.

The Good Fortune Kettle

The Good Fortune Kettle

ONCE UPON A TIME there lived a poor junkman, who one day found a badger caught in a trap. The old man felt sorry for the badger and straightway set it free.

The grateful badger in return wanted to help the poor junkman. So he turned himself into a teakettle and stealthily crawled into the basket the junkman was carrying on his back.

What a surprise the poor junk dealer received when he reached home after his day's work! Deep down in his junk basket he found a beautiful teakettle. In all his life he had never seen such a fine teakettle. He decided to take it to a certain temple priest who had always been very kind to him. He knew that the priest would want to buy such an unusual kettle.

Early the next morning, the junkman carried his treasure to the temple. As he expected, the priest was greatly pleased with the shining teakettle. The priest paid him three whole *ryo,* a far greater amount of money than the junkman could ever have dreamed of getting.

Amazed to have all this money, the junkman went home hardly believing his good fortune.

For a time the priest sat admiring his beautiful

teakettle. Then he filled it with water and put it on the fire to boil. Suddenly strange things began to happen.

The teakettle cried out, "It's hot! It's hot!" And with that, out came a badger's hairy head, four brown and hairy paws, and then a bushy tail! The badger-kettle hopped off the hearth and began to run round and round the room.

The priest was frightened. He did not intend to keep such a strange teakettle in his temple. He sent for the junkman and handed the kettle back to him.

Poor junkman! He had to carry the teakettle home, but he did not know what to do with it. At bedtime he placed it at the head of his bed.

At midnight a voice awakened him. He looked around, and finally discovered that it was coming from the teakettle.

"Dear old man," said the badger teakettle,

"yesterday you saved my life—for I am that badger you so kindly set free. I turned myself into a fine teakettle, for I wanted to help you earn some money. Why don't you carry me around with you now, to perform as a show? Together we could make a great many *ryo*."

The junkman decided to do just that. As he and the badger-kettle made their rounds of the villages, people flocked to see the dancing of the strange teakettle. To their delight, it could sing and walk a tightrope, as well as dance.

After many performances, the junkman was no longer poor, but rich—so wealthy, indeed, that he and the teakettle decided they could stop working and retire to a life of leisure.

Once more the junkman took his teakettle to the temple. He told his friend the priest how the badger he had set free had turned into this fine teakettle and helped him to make a fortune.

The priest was touched by the story of the faithful badger. This time he was delighted to accept the teakettle as a treasure to be cherished in the temple.

It is said today that the teakettle is still among the treasures of the Morinji Temple in the city of Tatebayashi.

The Tongue-Cut
Sparrow

The Tongue-Cut Sparrow

LONG, LONG AGO in Japan there lived an old man and an old woman. The old man was kindhearted and hard-working, but his wife had a scolding tongue that spoiled the happiness of their home. From morning to night she grumbled. For a long time the old man took no notice of her crossness. He spent most of the day at work in the fields or woods.

For his amusement, when he came home, the childless old man had a tame sparrow. He loved this little bird as much as if she were his child. After his hard day's work he would open the sparrow's cage and let her fly about the room. He would pet her, talk to her, and teach her little tricks, which she learned very quickly. He always saved for her a few tidbits from his supper.

One day when the old man had gone out to chop wood, the old woman turned to washing their clothes. When she went to get the starch she had prepared the day before, she found the bowl which she had filled yesterday quite empty.

While she stood wondering who could have taken the starch, down flew the pet sparrow. Bowing her feathered head—a trick which she had been taught by her master—the honest little bird confessed: "It is I who have taken the starch. I thought it was food put out for me, and I ate it all. I beg you to forgive me."

But the old woman was not willing to forgive. She had never loved the sparrow, and indeed had often complained to her husband about the extra work the small bird created. Now she was only too happy to find a reason to scold the pet. But she was not content with using harsh words. In a fit of rage she seized the sparrow and cut off her tongue.

"You took my starch with that tongue! Now you shall see what it is like to go without a tongue." With these words she drove the bird away, without the slightest pity for her suffering.

The old woman then prepared more rice starch, grumbling as she did so, and spread the starched clothes on boards to dry in the sun.

In the evening the old man came home, looking forward as usual to seeing his pet. But tonight the old man was to be disappointed.

Hastily he drew off his straw sandals and stepped onto the veranda. No sparrow was in sight. He called his wife and asked anxiously, "Where is *Suzume San* today? Where is Miss Sparrow?"

At first, the old woman pretended not to know.

"Your sparrow? I am sure I don't know. Come to think of it, I haven't seen her all afternoon. I shouldn't wonder if the ungrateful bird had flown away and left you."

But at last, when the old man gave her no peace and had asked her again and again, she confessed. She told him crossly how the sparrow had eaten the rice paste she had made for starching her clothes, and how when the sparrow had confessed, she had taken her scissors and cut off the sparrow's tongue. Finally, she had driven the bird away.

"How could you be so cruel? Oh! How could you be so cruel?" said the old man over and over.

"Poor Suzume San! She won't be able to sing

anymore. And the pain of the cutting must have made her ill. Is there nothing to be done?"

After his cross old wife had gone to sleep, the old man shed many tears. Then a bright thought comforted him. Tomorrow he would go look for the sparrow. At last he was able to fall asleep.

The next morning he rose early, as soon as the day broke, and snatching a hasty breakfast he started out over the hills and through the woods. At every clump of bamboos he stopped to cry, "Where, oh where, does my tongue-cut sparrow stay? Where, oh where, does my tongue-cut sparrow stay?"

He did not stop to rest for a noonday meal, but kept on far into the afternoon until he found himself near a large bamboo wood. There, sure enough, at the edge of the wood he saw his own dear sparrow waiting to welcome him. He ran forward joyfully to greet her. She bowed her little head and went through a number of the tricks her master had taught her, showing her pleasure at seeing her old friend again. And, wonderful to relate, she could talk as of old. The old man told her of his grief, but the sparrow begged him to think no more about the past, for she was quite well now.

In his joy the old man forgot how tired he was. His lost sparrow was found and she was well. He knew that she was no common bird; he would call her now the Lady Sparrow.

The Lady Sparrow asked the old man to follow her. Flying ahead, she led him to a beautiful house in the heart of the bamboo grove. The old man entered it in astonishment. It was built of the whitest wood. Its soft cream-colored mats were the finest he had ever seen, and the cushions that the sparrow brought out for him to sit on were made of the richest silk. Rare vases and lacquered boxes adorned the *tokonoma*, the alcove for precious objects, in each room.

The Lady Sparrow led the old man to the place of honor. Then, resting at a humble distance, she thanked him with polite bows for the kindness he had shown her for so many years. She introduced her family, and her lovely daughters brought in a feast so delicious that the old man thought he must be dreaming. In the middle of the dinner some of the daughters amused their guest by performing the *Suzume-odori,* the Sparrow's dance.

Never had the old man enjoyed himself so much. The hours flew by too quickly. The darkness of nighttime reminded him that his journey home was a long one and he must take his leave. He thanked his hostess for her splendid entertainment and begged her to forget all she had suffered. Now that he knew all was well with her, he could return home with a light heart. If ever she wanted him for anything, she had only to send for him and he would come at once.

The Lady Sparrow begged him to stay and rest, but the old man said he must return to his old wife—who would be cross because he had not come home at the usual time. Now that he knew where the Lady Sparrow lived, he would come to see her whenever he could spare the time.

Since the Lady Sparrow could not persuade him to stay longer, she gave an order to some of her servants, and at once they brought two wicker baskets—one heavy and the other light. These were placed before the old man, and the Lady Sparrow asked him to choose one of them for a present. The old man could not refuse and chose the lighter basket, saying, "I am now too old to carry the heavy basket."

The sparrows all helped to hoist the basket onto the old man's back and went to the gate to see him off, bidding him good-bye with many bows and entreating him to come again whenever he could.

At home, just as he expected, the old man found his wife even crosser than usual. It was late, and she had been waiting up for him.

"Where have you been all this time?" she shouted.

The old man tried to pacify her with the basket of presents. He told her of all that had happened, and how wonderfully he had been entertained at the sparrow's house.

"Let us see what is in the basket," said the old man, not giving her time to grumble again. "You must help me open it."

To their utter astonishment, they found the basket filled with gold and silver coins and precious jewels. The mats of their little cottage fairly glittered as they laid out the gifts and handled them over and over again. The old man was overjoyed. The riches would enable him to give up his hard work and live in ease the rest of his days.

"Thanks to my good little sparrow. Thanks to my good little sparrow," he repeated many times.

But the old woman, after her first surprise and satisfaction at the sight of the gold and silver, could not suppress the greed of her wicked nature. She began to reproach the old man for not having brought home the heavy basket of presents. In his innocence he had told her how he had refused the heavier one.

"You silly old man," she screamed. "Why did you not bring home the heavy basket. Think of what we have lost! We might have had twice as much silver and gold as this. You are certainly an old fool."

The old man wished that he had said nothing about the heavier one, but it was too late. The old woman, not content with the good luck which had so unexpectedly befallen them and which she so little deserved, made up her mind to get more if possible.

Early the next morning she made the old man describe the way to the sparrow's house. When he saw what was in her mind, he tried to keep her from going, but it was useless. Her greed made her forget her cruel treatment of the sparrow.

Ever since the Lady Sparrow had returned home in her sad plight, her family had talked about the old woman's wickedness. "How could she inflict so heavy a punishment for such an innocent offense?" They all loved the kind and patient old man, but they hated the old woman. If ever they had the chance, they would punish her as she deserved.

They had not long to wait.

After walking for several hours, the old woman at last found the bamboo grove which her husband had described. She stood before it and cried, "Where is the tongue-cut sparrow's house? Where is the tongue-cut sparrow's house?"

At last she noticed the eaves of the house sticking out from the bamboo foliage. She hastened to the door and knocked loudly.

When the servants told the Lady Sparrow that her old mistress was at the door asking to see her, she was indeed surprised. She wondered not a little at the boldness of the old woman in coming to the house. But the Lady Sparrow was polite. She went out to greet the visitor.

The old woman wasted no time. Without shame, she went right to the point.

"You need not trouble to entertain me as you did my old man. I have come to get the basket which he so stupidly left behind. I shall soon take my leave if you will give me the heavy basket. That is all I want."

The Lady Sparrow at once ordered her servants to bring out the heavy basket, which the old woman eagerly seized. She hoisted it onto her back, and, without stopping to thank the Lady Sparrow, hurried homeward.

The basket was so heavy that she could not walk fast. Often she had to sit down and rest. While she staggered along, her desire to open the basket grew greater and greater. Finally, the greedy old woman could wait no longer. She set the basket down by the wayside and opened it carefully, expecting to gloat over gold and silver and jewels.

What the old woman saw so terrified her that she nearly lost her senses. Horrible demons bounded out of the basket and surrounded her as if they intended to kill her. Not even in nightmares had she seen such frightful-looking creatures. A demon with one huge eye in the middle of its forehead glared at her; monsters with wide, gaping mouths opened them further as if to devour her; a huge snake began to coil and hiss; and a giant frog hopped toward her

croaking. Never had the old woman been so frightened. She ran from the spot as fast as her quaking legs would carry her. At home she fell to the floor in tears, and told her husband all that had happened to her.

She began to blame the sparrow, but the old man stopped her at once. "Don't blame the sparrow. It is your wickedness which has at last met its reward. I only hope this may be a lesson to you in the future."

The old woman said nothing more. From that day she repented. By degrees she became such a good old woman that her husband hardly knew her to be the same person. They lived their last days together happily, free from want or care, spending carefully the treasure the old man had received from his beloved pet, the tongue-cut sparrow.

Momotaro or
The Story of the Son
of a Peach

Momotaro or The Story of the Son of a Peach

LONG, LONG AGO there lived an old man and an old woman. They were poor country people and had to work hard to earn their daily rice. The old man cut firewood for the farmers around. While he was gone, the old woman, his wife, took care of the house and worked in their own little rice field.

One day the old man went to the hills as usual to cut wood, and the old woman went to the river to wash clothes.

It was nearly summer, and the country was very beautiful in its fresh greenness. The grass on the river banks looked like emerald velvet, and the pussy willows along the water's edge were shaking out soft spring tassels.

Breezes ruffled the smooth surface of the water. They touched the cheeks of the old couple who, for some reason they could not explain, felt very happy this morning.

The old woman at last found a clear space by the river and set down her basket of clothes. She began to scrub the garments one by one. The water was so clear that she could see tiny fish swimming to and fro and the bright pebbles at the bottom.

As she was busy at her washing, a great peach came bobbing down the stream. The old woman looked up. In all her life she had never seen such a big peach.

"How delicious that peach must be," she said to herself. "I must take it home to my old husband."

She stretched out her arm to grasp the peach, but it was quite beyond her reach. She looked about for a stick. Unfortunately, there was none near at hand. She knew that if she went off to look for one, she would lose the peach.

Stopping a moment to think what she would do, she remembered an old charm verse. She began to clap her hands in time with the bobbing of the peach down the stream. While she clapped, she sang this song:

> *Distant water is bitter,*
> *The near water is sweet;*
> *Pass by the distant water*
> *And come into the sweet.*

Strange to say, while she was repeating this little song, the peach drifted nearer and nearer. At last it stopped just in front of her so that she could lift it up in her hands. The old woman could not go on with her work, she was so happy and excited. She put all her clothes back into her bamboo basket, and with the basket on her back and the peach in her hand, she hurried homeward.

It seemed a long time to sunset, when her husband at last returned home. He carried a great bundle of wood on his back—so big that it all but hid him. He was tired and sometimes stopped to lean on his ax as he dragged along the path.

The old woman saw him coming and called out, "*Ojiisan!* Old Man! I have been waiting for you for such a long time today!"

"What is the matter? Why are you so impatient?" asked the old man, wondering at her unusual eagerness. "Has anything happened?"

"Oh, no. But I have found a present for you."

"Good," said the old man. He washed his feet in a basin of water and stepped up to the veranda.

The old woman ran inside the house and brought out the big peach. It seemed even heavier than before. She held it up to him, saying, "Just look at this! Did you ever see such a great peach?"

The old man was astonished. "This is indeed the largest peach I have ever seen! Wherever did you get it?"

"I found it in the river where I was washing," answered the old woman. And she told him the whole story.

"I am very glad that you have found it. Let us eat it now, for I am hungry," said Ojiisan.

He brought out their kitchen knife and was about to cut the peach in two when, wonderful to tell, the peach split apart by itself, and a clear voice sounded, "Wait a bit, old man." And out of the peach stepped a beautiful little baby.

The old man and woman were both so astonished that they fell to the ground. The baby spoke again:

"Don't be afraid. I am no demon or fairy. I will tell you the truth. Heaven has had compassion on you. Every day and every night you have lamented that you had no child. Your cry has been heard, and I am sent to be the son of your old age."

On hearing this, the old man and woman were happy indeed. Night and day they had cried out their sorrow at having no child to bring happiness to them in their lonely old age, and now that their prayer was answered they were nearly overcome with joy. The old man took the baby in his arms, and then the old woman did the same. They named him Momotaro, or Son of a Peach, because of the way he had come to them.

The years passed by quickly. When the child had grown to be fifteen years of age, he was taller and far stronger than other boys of his years. He had a handsome face and a heart full of courage, and he was unusually wise for his age. The old couple delighted in looking at him, for he was just what they thought a hero should be.

One day Momotaro came to his foster parents and said solemnly:

"Your goodness to me has been higher than the mountain and deeper than the sea. I do not know how to thank you enough."

"Why," answered the old man, "it is a matter of course that parents should bring up their son. When you are older, it will be your turn to take care of us."

"I hope you will be patient with me," said Momotaro. "I have a request which I hope you will grant me. I want to go away for a time."

"Where do you wish to go?"

"Far away in the Northeast there is an island which is the stronghold of a band of devils. I have heard how they invade our land and kill and rob the people. They are disloyal to our Emperor and disobey his laws. I must go and conquer them, and bring back the plunder they have taken."

The old man and his wife were surprised to hear all this from a boy of only fifteen years. But they thought it best to let Momotaro go, since he was strong and fearless. Indeed he was no common child but had been sent as a gift from Heaven.

"Go to the island," said the old man to Momotaro. "Destroy the demons and bring peace to our land."

The old man and woman at once set to work to pound millet seeds in the kitchen mortar, for Momotaro would need dumplings to eat on his journey.

At last the dumplings were made, and Momotaro was ready to start on his long journey.

The parting was sad. The eyes of the two old people filled with tears and their voices trembled as they said: "Go with all care and speed. We expect you to come back a victor."

In silence the eyes of Momotaro and his parents met in farewell.

Momotaro now strode rapidly on his way. He kept on until midday, when he began to feel hungry, so he sat down under a tree and opened his bag. He had just begun to eat one of the dumplings when out from the high grass by the roadside came a dog almost as large as a colt. It made straight for Momotaro and asked who he was.

Momotaro laughed. "You do not know who I am? I am Momotaro, and I am on my way to overcome the devils on their island."

The dog then bowed so low that his forehead touched the ground.

"Are you Momotaro? I have heard of your great strength. Are you indeed on your way to invade the Island of Devils? If you will take me with you, I shall be grateful to become one of your followers."

"I will take you, if you wish to go," said Momotaro.

"Thank you!" said the dog. "And now will you give me one of your dumplings?"

"They are the best kind in Japan," said Momotaro. "I cannot spare you a whole one; but I will give you half of one."

"Thank you," said the dog, taking the piece thrown to him.

After Momotaro and the dog had walked over many hills and through many valleys, a monkey swung down from a tree beside the road and greeted them.

"Good morning, Momotaro! You are welcome in this part of the country. I am glad to see you and should like to travel with you, if you will allow me to."

Momotaro asked the monkey, "Who are you?"

"I live in these hills and have heard of your journey to the Island of Devils. Nothing would please me more than to follow you."

"You wish to go to the Island of Devils and fight with me?"

"Yes, I do indeed," replied the monkey.

"Come along then," said Momotaro and he gave the monkey half a dumpling.

Momotaro sent the dog on ahead with a flag and ordered the monkey to march behind with a sword. He walked between them carrying a war fan made of iron.

By and by the three came to a large field where a most beautiful bird flew down before them. Its body feathers were of five different colors, and its head wore a scarlet cap.

The bird begged to be taken into Momotaro's company. "I am a poor creature called a pheasant. Please allow me to follow you behind the dog and the monkey!"

Momotaro saw that the pheasant would make a good fighter. He asked it to join the company and gave it, also, half a dumpling.

Momotaro's power over the three grew great and they all became good friends.

Hurrying on day after day they at last came to the shore of the Northeastern Sea. But as far as they could see there was no sign of an island. All that broke the stillness was the rolling of the waves upon the shore.

Now the dog and the monkey and the pheasant had come very bravely through the long valleys and over the high hills. But they had never seen the sea before and for the first time since they had set out they were bewildered.

They gazed at each other in silence. How were they to cross the water and reach the Island of Devils?

Momotaro saw that they were daunted by the sight of the sea and to test them he cried out, "Why do you hesitate? Are you afraid of the sea? What cowards you are! It will be far better for me to go alone. I discharge you all at once."

The three animals then clung to Momotaro's sleeve and begged him not to send them away.

"We are not afraid of the sea," said the monkey.

"Please take us with you!" said the pheasant.

"Yes, please," said the dog.

Seeing that they had gained a little courage, Momotaro said, "Well, then, I will take you with me, but be careful."

After a time, Momotaro located a small ship and took them all aboard. With fair wind and weather the ship moved like an arrow over the sea. At first the dog, the monkey, and the pheasant were frightened by the waves and the rolling of the vessel, but they became accustomed to the water and began to look eagerly for the demons' island. Since the wind blew in their favor and they met no storms, the ship made a quick voyage. Soon, in bright sunshine, they spied land.

Momotaro knew at once that what they saw was the monsters' stronghold. On top of the island, looking out to sea, sat a large castle. Momotaro looked up at it and wondered how he should begin his attack. His three followers watched him, waiting for orders. At last he called to the pheasant:

"It is lucky that we have you with us, for you have good wings. You must fly at once to the castle and engage the demons in fighting. We shall follow you."

The pheasant at once flew off from the ship, beating the air gladly with his wings. He took up a position on the castle roof and called out, "All you monsters, hear me. The great Japanese general Momotaro has come to take your stronghold. If you wish to save your lives, you must surrender at once and break off the horns that grow on your foreheads. Otherwise, we, the pheasant, the dog, and the monkey, will kill you all."

The horned demons looked up. Seeing only a pheasant, they laughed.

"A wild pheasant, indeed. It is ridiculous to hear such words from a poor thing like you. Wait till you get a blow from one of our iron bars."

Angry indeed were the devils. They shook their horns and their shocks of red hair fiercely. They ran at the pheasant to knock him down with their iron bars. But the pheasant flew to one side to escape their blows and attacked one and then another on the head. Round and round he flew, beating the air so wildly that the devils wondered whether they had one or many birds to fight.

In the meantime, Momotaro had brought his ship to land. He saw that the shore was steep and that the large fortified castle was surrounded by high walls and large iron gates.

Hoping to find some way of entering, he walked up a path, followed by the monkey and the dog. They came to a little low door in the castle wall—a door so small that Momotaro could hardly crawl through it.

The pheasant, who was all this time fighting hard, saw Momotaro and his little band pushing in there at the back of the castle.

Momotaro and the dog and the monkey now also attacked the devils so furiously that the devils could not stand against them. The monsters were routed, for the four fought like a hundred, so strong were they, and so brave. Some of the devils fell off the parapet of the castle to the rocks beneath; others fell into the sea.

At last the chief of the devils was the only one left, and he saw that he must surrender. Humbly he threw down his iron bar before Momotaro, and broke off his horns in a token of submission.

"I cannot stand against you. If you will spare my life, I will give you the treasure hidden in this castle."

Momotaro answered, "I cannot spare your wicked life, however much you beg, for you have killed and tortured many people and robbed our country for many years."

Momotaro tied up the devil chief and gave him into the monkey's charge. Then he set the castle prisoners free and gathered together the treasure. With the dog and the pheasant carrying this plunder, Momotaro made a triumphant journey home.

Those whom the wicked demon had carried off to be his slaves were returned safely to their homes.

Momotaro was treated as a great hero, which made the old couple's joy in him greater than ever. The treasure enabled them all to live in peace and plenty to the end of their days.

The White Hare
and the Crocodiles

The White Hare
and the Crocodiles

LONG, LONG AGO there lived in Japan a little white hare. His home was on the island of Oki, just across the sea from Inaba, a province on the mainland.

Now the hare wanted very much to cross over to the mainland. Day after day he would sit on the shore, looking longingly over the water and hoping to find some way of crossing it.

One day, when the hare was looking out as usual, he saw a great crocodile swimming near his island.

"This is very lucky!" thought the hare. "Now I shall be able to get my wish. I shall ask the crocodile to carry me across the sea!"

But he was doubtful whether the crocodile would consent to do this. So he decided that, instead of asking a favor, he would try to get what he wanted by trickery.

In a loud voice he called to the crocodile, "Oh, Mr. Crocodile, isn't it a lovely day?"

The crocodile swam nearer the shore, very pleased to hear a voice. He had come out all by himself that day to enjoy the bright sunshine, and was just beginning to feel a bit lonely when the hare's cheerful greeting broke the silence.

"I wonder who it was that spoke to me just now. Was it you, Mr. Hare? You must be lonely all by yourself."

"Oh, no, I am not at all lonely," said the hare. "It is such a fine day that I just came out on the beach to enjoy myself. Won't you stop awhile and play with me?"

The crocodile pulled himself out of the sea, and the two played games together for some time. Then the hare said, "Mr. Crocodile, you live in the sea and I live on this island, and we do not often meet, so I know very little about you. Tell me, do you think the number of crocodiles is greater than the number of hares?"

"Of course, there are more crocodiles than hares," answered the crocodile. "Can you not see that for yourself? You live on this small island, while I live in the sea, which spreads through all parts of the world. If I should call together all the crocodiles who dwell in the sea, you hares would be as nothing compared to us!" The crocodile sounded very conceited.

The hare, who meant to play a trick on the

crocodile, answered, "Do you think it possible for you to call up enough crocodiles to form a line from this island across the sea to Inaba?"

The crocodile thought for a moment.

"Of course, it is possible."

"Then do try," said the artful hare, "and I will count the number from here."

The crocodile, who was simple-minded and hadn't the least idea that the hare intended to play a trick on him, agreed to do what the hare asked.

"Wait a moment, while I go back into the sea and call my company together."

The crocodile plunged into the sea and was gone for some time. The hare, meanwhile, waited patiently on the shore. At last the crocodile appeared, bringing with him a large number of other crocodiles.

"Look, Mr. Hare!" said the crocodile. "It is nothing for my friends to form a line between here and Inaba. There are enough crocodiles to stretch even as far as China or India. Did you ever see so many crocodiles?"

The whole company of crocodiles then arranged themselves in the water so as to form a bridge between the island of Oki and the mainland of Inaba. When the hare saw the bridge of crocodiles, he said, "How splendid! I did not believe this was possible. Now let me count you all. To do this, however, with your permission I must walk on your backs over to the other side, so please be so good as not to move, or else I shall fall into the sea and be drowned."

The hare hopped off the island onto the strange bridge of crocodiles, counting as he jumped from one crocodile's back to another's.

"Please keep quite still, or I shall not be able to count. One, two, three, four, five, six, seven, eight, nine . . ."

Thus the cunning hare walked right across to

the mainland of Inaba. Not content with getting his wish, he now began to jeer at the crocodiles instead of thanking them. As he leaped off the last one's back, he said, "Oh, you stupid crocodiles, now I have done with you!"

He aimed to run away as fast as he could, but he did not escape so easily. As soon as the crocodiles understood that the hare had played a trick on them to enable him to cross the sea, and that he was now laughing at them for their stupidity, they became angry and determined to take revenge. They ran after the hare and caught him. Then they surrounded the poor little animal and pulled out all his fur. He begged them to spare him and cried out loudly, but with each tuft of his fur they pulled out, the crocodiles said, "This serves you right."

When the crocodiles had pulled out the last bit of fur, they threw the poor hare onto the beach and swam away, laughing at what they had done.

The hare was now a pitiful sight. His beautiful white fur was gone, and his bare little body quivered with pain. He lay on the beach and wept for his misfortune. Although his suffering was due to his own trickery, no one could help feeling sorry for him. The crocodiles had been cruel indeed.

At this moment a number of youths arrayed like king's sons happened to pass by. Seeing the hare lying there on the beach crying, they asked him what the matter was.

The hare lifted up his head from between his paws and said, "I had a fight with some crocodiles, but I was beaten. They pulled out all my fur and left me here to suffer—that is why I am crying."

One of the young men pretended kindness, and said to the hare, "I feel sorry for you, and I know of a remedy which will cure your sore body. You must bathe in the sea, and then sit in the wind. This will make your fur grow again, and you will be just as you were before."

The young men went on, leaving the hare very pleased to think he had found a cure. At once he bathed in the sea and then sat where the wind could blow upon him.

But as the breezes blew and dried him, the hare's skin became tight and it stiffened. And the salt from the sea water increased the pain so greatly that he rolled on the sand in agony and cried aloud.

Just then another young man passed by, carrying a great bag on his back. He saw the hare, and asked why he was crying so loudly.

The poor hare, remembering how he had been deceived by one very like the man who now spoke to him, did not answer, but continued to cry.

This man, however, had a kind heart. He looked

at the hare pityingly, and said, "You poor thing. I see that your fur has been all pulled out and your skin is quite bare. Who can have treated you so cruelly?"

When the hare heard these kind words, he was encouraged and told the man all that had befallen him. The little animal hid nothing from his friend, but confessed how he had played a trick on the crocodiles and had jeered at them for their stupidity. Then he told how the crocodiles had revenged themselves on him, and how he had been fooled by a party of young men who looked very like his new kind friend. The hare ended his tale of woe by begging the man to give him medicine that would make his fur grow again.

The man looked down at the hare. "I am very sorry for all you have suffered, but you must remember that it was only the result of your deceit."

"I know," answered the sorrowful hare, "but I

have repented and made up my mind never to be deceitful again. I beg you to tell me how I may cure my sore body and make my fur grow again."

"I will help you," said the man. "First, you must bathe well in that pond of fresh water over there, and wash away all the salt. Next you must pick some of those *gama* spikes from bulrushes growing near the edge of the water, spread them on the ground, and roll yourself on them. If you will do this, your fur will grow again, and you will be quite well again in only a little while."

The hare was delighted to be told in such a kindly way exactly what he must do. He crawled over to the pond and bathed himself carefully. He picked the *gama* spikes and rolled himself over the blossoms.

To his amazement, even as he was doing this, the hare saw fine white fur begin to grow again on his body. His pain soon ceased and he felt just as usual.

Hopping joyfully over to his benefactor and kneeling at his feet, the hare looked up.

"I cannot express my thanks well enough for all you have done for me. It is my earnest wish to do something for you in return. Please tell me who you are."

"I am no king's son as you think but a great great-great-grandson of the younger brother of the Sun Goddess. My name is Okuni-nushi-no-Mikoto," answered the man. "Those beings who passed here before me are my half-brothers. They have heard of a beautiful princess called Yakami who lives in this province of Inaba, and they are on their way to find her and to ask her to marry one of them. On this journey I am only an attendant, so I walk behind them with this great bag on my back."

Humbling himself before this great being, the hare replied, "It is impossible to believe that the unkind fellow who sent me to bathe in the sea is one of your brothers. I am quite sure that the Princess will refuse to become the bride of any one of them. She will prefer you for your goodness of heart."

Okuni now bid the little animal good-bye and, going quickly on his way, soon overtook his brothers—just as they were entering the Princess's gate.

Exactly as the hare had predicted, the Princess would not be persuaded to become the bride of any of the brothers. But when she looked at the kind young man who was a great-great-great-grandson of the younger brother of the Sun Goddess, she went straight up to him and said, "It is to you I wish to be wed."

Thus it came about that Okuni and the Princess called Yakami were married. The hare became famous as "The White Hare of Inaba," but what became of the crocodiles nobody knows.

About This Series

IN RECENT DECADES, folk tales and fairy tales from all corners of the earth have been made available in a variety of handsome collections and in lavishly illustrated picture books. But in the 1950s, such a rich selection was not yet available. The classic fairy and folk tales were most often found in cumbersome books with small print and few illustrations. Helen Jones, then children's book editor at Little, Brown and Company, accepted a proposal from a Boston librarian for an ambitious series with a simple goal — to put an international selection of stories into the hands of children. The tales would be published in slim volumes, with wide margins and ample leading, and illustrated by a cast of contemporary artists. The result was a unique series of books intended for children to read by themselves — the Favorite Fairy Tales series. Available only in hardcover for many years, the books have now been reissued in paperbacks that feature new illustrations and covers.

The series embraces the stories of sixteen different

countries: France, England, Germany, India, Ireland, Sweden, Poland, Russia, Spain, Czechoslovakia, Scotland, Denmark, Japan, Greece, Italy, and Norway. Some of these stories may seem violent or fantastical to our modern sensibilities, yet they often reflect the deepest yearnings and imaginings of the human mind and heart.

Virginia Haviland traveled abroad frequently and was able to draw upon librarians, storytellers, and writers in countries as far away as Japan to help make her selections. But she was also an avid researcher with a keen interest in rare books, and most of the stories she included in the series were found through a diligent search of old collections. Ms. Haviland was associated with the Boston Public Library for nearly thirty years—as a children's and branch librarian, and eventually as Readers Advisor to Children. She reviewed for *The Horn Book Magazine* for almost thirty years and in 1963 was named Head of the Children's Book Section of the Library of Congress. Ms. Haviland remained with the Library of Congress for nearly twenty years and wrote and lectured about children's literature throughout her career. She died in 1988.